INCREDIBLY

by
Jacques-Olivier Baruch

Series director :
François Cherrier

FAST

new
Discovery
B O O K S
New York

Faster than the eye

In 1883 the physiologist Étienne Jules Marey used photography to analyze the movement of a man walking. To eliminate any extraneous information, he dressed his model in black and white so that the figure appears alone on the black background of the photographic plate.

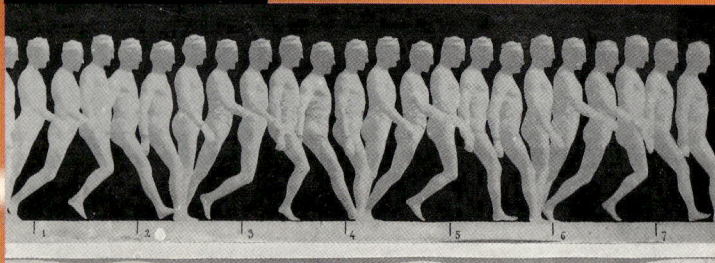

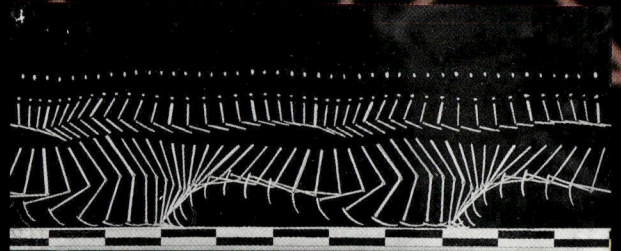

Magical, incredible, otherworldly: A multitude of adjectives exist to describe the sensation of watching a slow-motion film of a bird in flight, an insect fluttering, or a bullet hitting a target. All these phenomena last no more than several thousandths of a second and are totally outside our range of vision. Our retina can capture a wealth of details but cannot register movement beyond a certain speed. Our brains no longer receive information faster than 1/24th of a second. The blurred image is the reality that transmits a sensation of speed to the viewer. Photography, motion pictures, high-speed video, and even more sophisticated techniques exist to trap time: These constitute our artificial vision, our references, and our tools to research everything that is too fast to see. With them, we can break down, analyze, understand, or correct a movement and fully experience this astonishing world of speed.

71

Other tools for other time frames. A "stick" figure is created by optic sensors (the white marks placed on the joints of a runner) and a computer connected to a high-speed video camera. The runner's stride can be analyzed in real time.

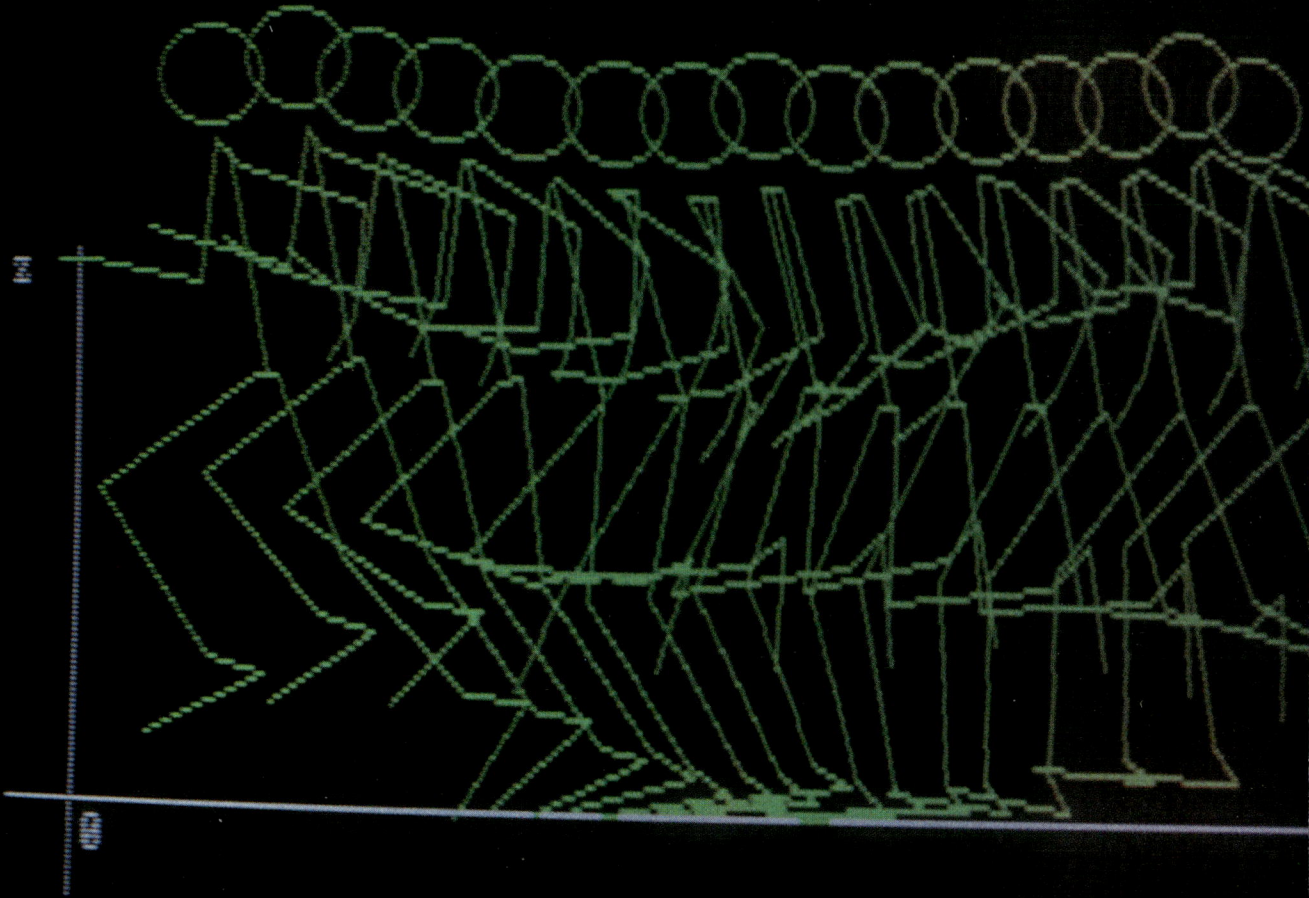

Made in Finland

TIME FROZEN IN A SINGLE FRAME

Time is impalpable. Nevertheless, we have been able to record it since the 19th century. Photographers juggle with the film speed and the exposure time (or the speed of the flash illuminating the subject) to capture this fleeting phenomenon. Joseph Nicéphore Niepce, inventor of photography, did not use his camera to freeze a moment in time. He couldn't. In 1826 his photographic plate was covered with Judean bitumen. The exposure time was so slow that his models had to remain perfectly still for several hours. There

was no point, therefore, in photographing moving subjects. In 1839 William Henry Fox Talbot invented the technique of printing photographs on paper and reduced exposure times to 30 seconds. In the 1850s, exposure times finally dropped to less than one second, and in 1888 George Eastman launched the first Kodak with a shutter speed of 1/20th of a second. This speed, available on cameras today, is still too slow to capture subjects in action. The "don't move!" order was primarily meant for human subjects. Motion is a series of

positions, and several images have to be taken at regular intervals to reproduce it. In 1883 Frenchman Etienne Jules Marey invented a "photographic gun," while in the United States, Eadweard Muybridge set up a series of cameras to capture the movement of a galloping horse. The results were remarkable for the time. Marey and Muybridge could not have known that they had invented the techniques of filmmaking.

By breaking down the flight of a pelican into individual images with his photographic gun, Etienne Jules Marey, physiologist and inventor, became one of the founders of movies.

Movement is fleeting to the human eye, but man has other resources. He can use machines to extend the boundaries of his own perception. Sophisticated cameras with extremely short exposure times can produce clear images of high-speed scenes. Photography has become a sort of visual memory of humanity and a tool for understanding. Marey used it for this purpose, and instead of trying to reconstruct a particular movement, he analyzed the movement of living subjects.

Every movement has elegance and function.

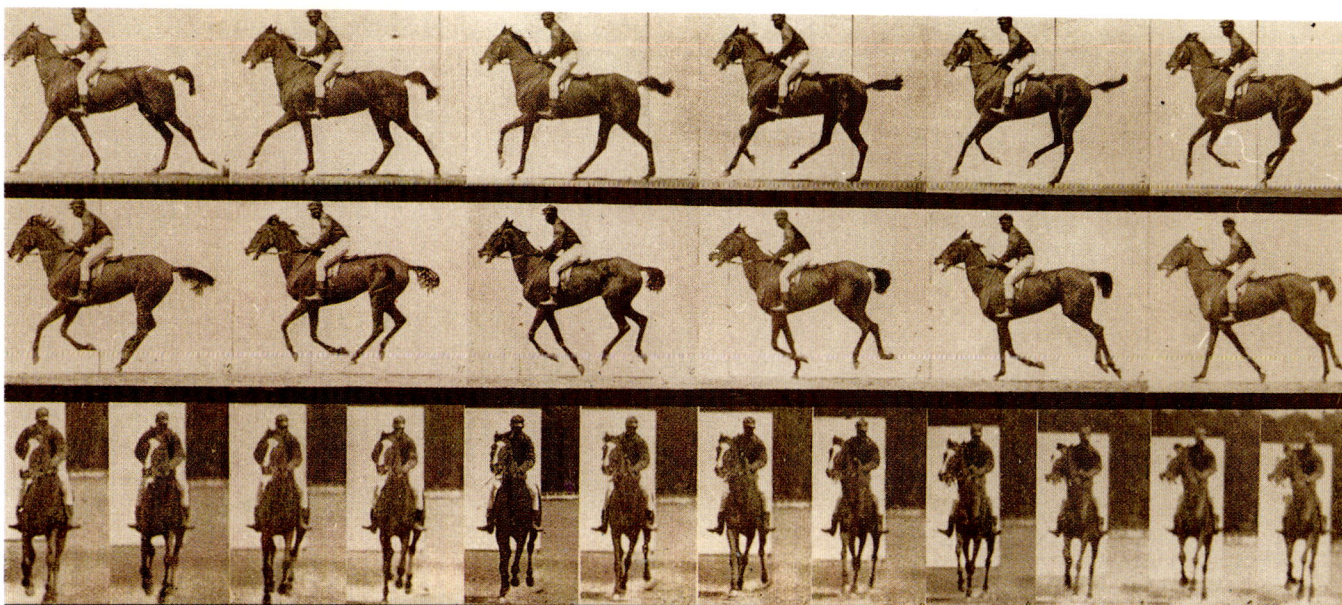

Elegance can be admired—function, understood.

An event filmed in slow motion

Entirely new worlds can be discovered using various photographic techniques. Two separate time frames seem to coexist: the time we can see with our own eyes and that of our "artificial" vision. By placing an entire sequence in a single image or by slowing down moving images, each phase of the movement becomes accessible. Strobe lights, electronic traps, and high-speed film and video cameras: Every visual researcher develops his own instruments to observe high-speed motion.

A cat always lands on its feet, no matter how it is dropped. Before Muybridge or Marey, nobody had been able to verify this truism, and illustrations of the movement were often incorrect. A cat does not turn around in a single movement. It first twists its front paws around, then, through an incredible contortion of its body, manages to pull its back paws around. It then arches its back to cushion the landing.

FAST AS A CAMERA FLASH

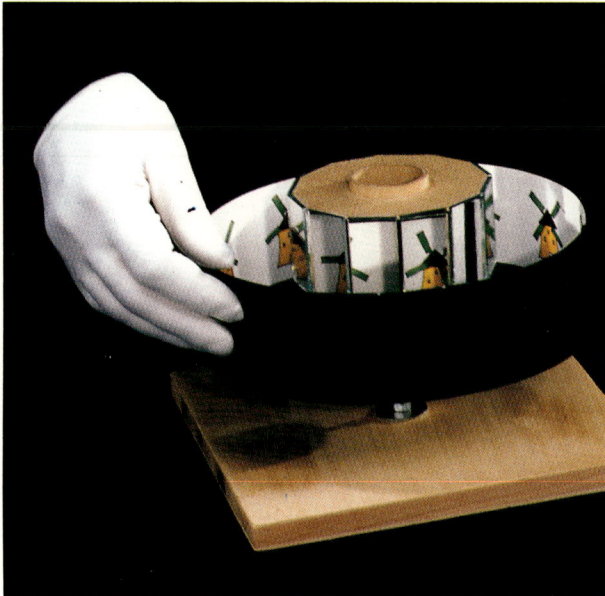

A film is merely a series of still images connected end to end. The illusion of continuous movement is due to the phenomenon of persistence of vision; in other words, images remain on our retina for approximately one-third of a second. The praxinoscope, invented in 1877 by Emile Reynaud, animated fixed images. This machine was the last of its kind invented before the development of cinematography in 1895 by the Lumière brothers in France.

In dance clubs strobe lights flash in synch to the rhythm of the music. Dancers appear to be frozen with each illumination. Photographers were quick to adopt this technique to their own purposes. In the United States Professor Harold Edgerton of MIT (Massachusetts Institute of Technology) was the first to use it in the 1930s. By accelerating the rhythm of the flashes, he could capture faster movements. Marey used a different technique: He attached a disk to the front of his camera in the place of the shutter; this disk had a series of slots drilled into it. He turned it with a crank, and each time a slot passed in front of the lens (at a speed of 1/500th of a second), the film recorded

To reveal the motion of a bouncing ball, the film is exposed many times, but only for an extremely brief moment. Two techniques can be used: a disk shutter placed in front of the camera or a rapid succession of flashes. Both produce an image of the different phases of an event in a single photograph.

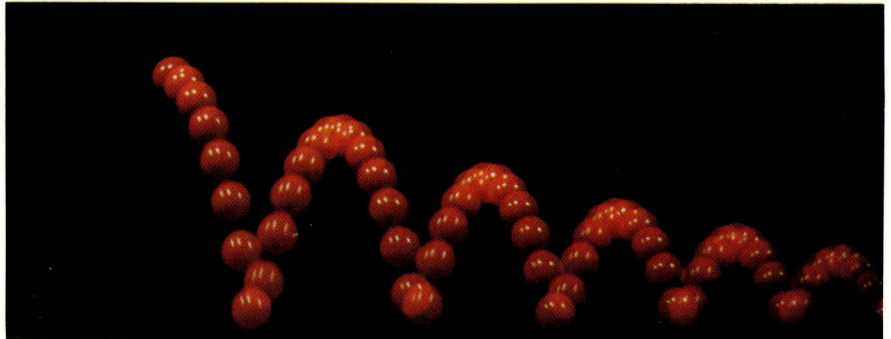

an image. He named this technique photochronography, as he believed that the photograph was only the medium or trace of the movement itself. The 1889 International Congress of Photography changed the term, calling the technique chronophotography instead. With the advent of strobe lights and multiple flashes and these slotted shutters, the number of subjects multiplied. Suddenly, films were taken of everything that moved. Marey captured the flights of birds, including pigeons, sea gulls, herons, and even a pelican. His studies of animal flight contributed to airplane research and development.

Harold Edgerton invented the strobe light, which creates a series of brief illuminations. For this photograph, however, he could not interfere with his subject. He had to be careful not to blind pole-vaulter David Tork in this photograph taken in 1964 in Boston Garden. He therefore placed the flash at a comfortable distance from the athlete, but he increased its power.

TAKING TO THE AIR

The majestic flight of birds is a precisely engineered event. Each part of a bird's body contributes to the action—with varying degrees of success. Everything depends on the ratio between its body weight and the surface area of its wings. When this ratio is unfavorable, its takeoff resembles the slow and cumbersome movement of certain cargo planes. A bird then has to run a good distance before it can manage to lift up its feet. It bounces several times to increase its speed and to create a sufficient pressure difference between the underside of the wing and the top side. The wings of birds create a "bearing surface," while the propulsion is created by flapping. Birds control the direction of flight with their tails. Herons and waders use their wings as parachutes.

Most birds flap their wings to fly: The wings describe figure eights in the sky just like airplane propellers. Bats, which can reach speeds of up to 30 mph, are fast, but are not the fastest animals in the sky; wild geese can travel 62 mph and falcons 124 mph. Each species flaps its wings at a different rate. The heron flaps them twice a second, the pigeon ten times, the hummingbird eighty times. Insects are even faster: Flies flap their wings 200 times a second and gnats up to 1,000 times!

A photographer must have a large store of patience to capture these memorable images. He sets up his equipment—multiple flashes or strobe lights—in a place often used by the bird, generally near the nest or near prey.

Scientists can obtain films of longer movements by factoring in the wind speed and the physical capacities of the bird.

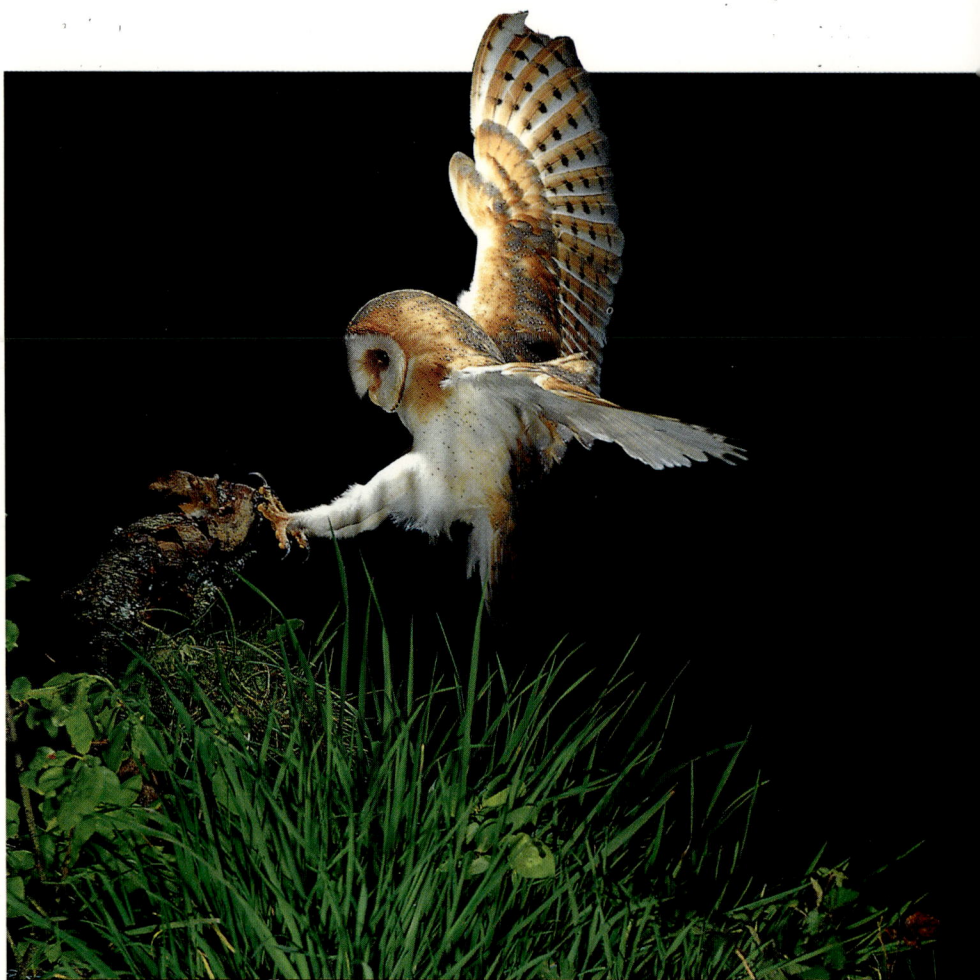

Nocturnal birds are not difficult to photograph. They must merely be forced to follow a certain trajectory. To capture the moment when an owl lands to catch its prey means that the photographer must know the takeoff point. He must then position the prey in the right place. The flash equipment is set according to the exposure time.

These creatures of the night are not birds; they are mammals. The flight pattern of bats is similar to that of birds but is less regular. Some bats are no larger than 6 inches, while the largest measures up to 5 feet across. Their wings consist of skin stretched between extraordinarily long fingers.

There is more than one way to take to the air.

THE HIDDEN MECHANISM OF AN ANIMAL'S LEAP

An animal's weight is not an important element in a jump. The earth's gravity is the same for everyone and everything. If a small animal wants to jump 8 inches, it must leave the ground at a speed of 6.5 feet per second, approximately 4.3 mph. If it wants to jump 8 feet, its initial speed must be 23 feet per second, or 15.5 mph. The animal's muscular system is of the utmost importance. The marvelous mechanism of various animals can be analyzed by capturing their jumps using the techniques of chronophotography or the "photographic gun." But it is not easy to catch wild animals in flight. The quality of the image depends on many variables, the first of which is the speed of the jump. For a clear image, the exposure time must be properly adapted to the movement. This requirement often creates a lighting problem. The faster a subject moves, the brighter the light must be to expose the film correctly. All these variables are carefully calculated to create the ideal photograph. Most photographs are made in a studio, not outdoors. Albert Visage, who photographed these field mice, took six months to obtain his chronophotography. He first had to catch wild field mice and create an environment similar to that of their natural habitat; otherwise, they would not reproduce. Another problem: Field mice are ferocious and kill one another. One month after the birth of the first babies, he had to isolate them and start the taming process all over again. To photograph them, he constructed a small island surrounded by a pond. He placed a cage containing food on the opposite bank. When his equipment was ready, the lighting set up, and the film loaded in the camera, he waited until the field mice jumped from the island to the cage, which they invariably did, occasionally falling in the pond in the process. Many animals—insects, birds, and mammals—jump, but none with the agility, speed, and grace of the frog.

Photographers capturing speed often require special equipment, which is not easy to use outside. They all prefer to work in mini-studios so that they can control every aspect of the shot. They have to reconstruct a natural environment and "direct" the animals, as in this photograph of a weasel chasing a field mouse.

This field mouse has been caught in midflight. The photographer waited until the mouse tried to jump over a pool of water to reach some food, then filmed each stage of the jump using a special camera.

There are not many ways to fly in the air.

A TIME FOR EVERYTHING

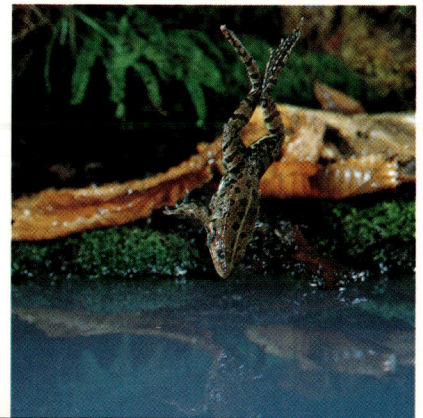

One-tenth of a second later . . .   and the moment is gone.

Photographs freeze time and stop motion. Several images are required to record movement, which can be broken down into an infinite number of sequences. The appearance of a subject changes completely when it is filmed in a different time frame.

In photographs from the 19th century, for which the subject had to remain motionless for at least ten minutes, many details appear out of focus. Shots taken at 1/60th of a second produce a clear image, but a closer examination reveals that hair has moved and is blurred, the subject blinked, or a hand trembled. As for a frog, it would have left the frame long before the photograph was finished!

Each exposure time must be adapted to the subject and must be as brief as the movement. When a frog jumps in the water or catches a fly, it needs only 1/10th of a second to extend its back legs and jump several times its own height. At the same time, it retracts its eyes into their sockets to protect them, then curls up to cushion the landing in the water. These movements are so fast that even if the photographer set the exposure speed to 1/20th of a second, the frog would leave nothing more than a blurred image. The distance between the camera and the subject is also, of course, a determining factor.

The photographer's preparatory work consists of finding the precise setting for the speed of the action, the exposure time, and the time between each photograph. He usually uses a motor drive mounted on the camera to advance the film. Yet this technique has limitations. It does not produce a chronophotograph (which captures the entire scene on the same image), and the motor drive is often too slow for certain scenes. An electronic clock is now often used. It can synchronize the different flash devices set up for the chronophotograph to within one-billionth of a second, if needed. It also triggers the other cameras set up to photograph the event.

Another problem involves the shutter speed. In most modern cameras, this speed can be set from a few seconds to 1/1,000th of a second. Certain professional cameras can even shoot pictures at 1/4,000th of a second. Anything faster raises the problem of advancing the film quickly enough. The gears can no longer function properly at these speeds. The various mechanisms are not synchronized, and beyond a certain threshold, the tension becomes too high and the film breaks.

For certain shots, single frame cameras are replaced by high-speed video or movie cameras. These integrate new techniques and are capable of filming several million frames per second. Unfortunately, these images do not have the same quality as a photograph.

Patience. The universe changes with each time frame. The photographer adapts to these conditions by repeating a scene again and again until he is rewarded with the image he seeks.

Every animal adapts to its environment to ensure its own survival. Eating requires that an animal's reaction time be faster than that of its prey. And to stay out of the mouth and belly of another animal, an animal must act more quickly than its predator. Animal photographers have come to understand this ruthless world. They adjust the camera's shutter speed and the length of time between photographs to the requirements of each particular animal. They can then capture an entire scene. One last requirement: unshakable patience.

FASTER AND FASTER!

Some movement is too fast for even a camera to capture, but not for high-speed video and movie cameras. Their capacities are almost inconceivable: They can freeze objects flying at more than 6,200 mph.

The shutter speed of a camera depends on mechanical limitations. Video systems, designed on electronic circuits, can attain exposure times of several nanoseconds (several billionths of a second). The Ballistic Range Camera SV-553 by Hadland, a company that specializes in missile firings, can take from one to sixteen images of a missile in flight and display them almost in real time, a mere half-second later. This possibility of high-speed analysis is the major advantage of high-speed video cameras.

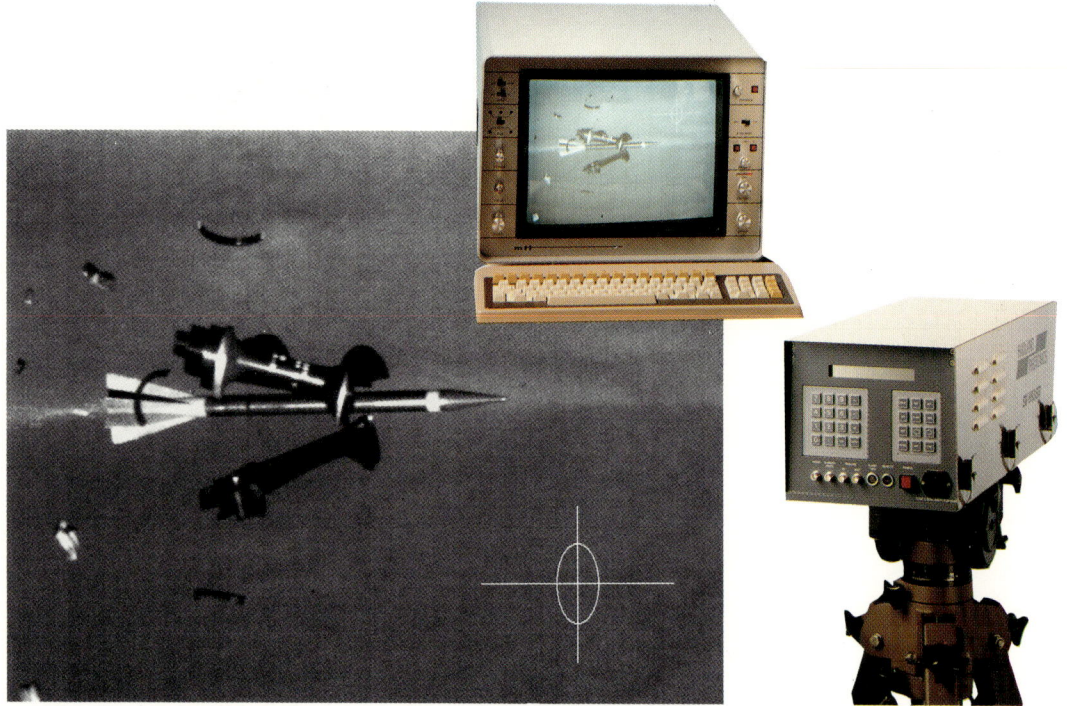

A photograph captures a brief moment of the present, saving it for eternity. Standard cameras cannot operate at speeds of several hundreds of microseconds. Movie or video cameras can be used, provided the internal mechanism is well stabilized. Due to the tension exerted on the film by the drive mechanism, a speed of more than 500 frames per second would tear the film irreparably.

This type of equipment is called an intermittent camera, and it is more than sufficient to record many events, such as the flight and return of a boomerang, impact measurements, and animals in action.

Special cameras have been developed for faster events. The film does not advance frame by frame, but runs continuously through the film gate. A prism turns at the same speed so that the image is not distorted. These cameras can film up to 40,000 frames per second.

Video cameras connected directly to computers can do much better still. These do not look anything like normal cameras; they consist of an array of light sensors in which the charge is directly digitized and recorded. The current record is 60 million frames per second!

Industry has understood the possibilities offered by video cameras. They have a capacity to analyze high-speed events almost in real time. Problems that arise in industrial assembly lines—incorrect designs or faulty assembly—can be solved quickly.

The HSV-1000 camera by the Japanese firm Nac flashes every 10 microseconds. It can film at a rate of 10,000 frames per second for 15 minutes. These images are stored in a video recording device, displayed on a color monitor, and can be analyzed in real time by a microcomputer.

To within one-billionth of a second

PHYSICAL MYSTERIES

Viewed from the perspective of a high-speed camera, common events become surprisingly beautiful. A marble falling into water resembles a meteorite dropping to earth, creating a crater that erosion will obliterate in a few million years. With a marble, however, the impact lasts less than one-tenth of a second and disappears almost as fast.

Most events cannot be described simply. Theorists look for universal laws. Observers invent their own instruments. They verify the theories, and through their discoveries of inexplicable events, they add a piece to the puzzle of the universe. A marble falls into the water, creating an impact between a hard body and a soft one. The simplest explanation is that it falls in and drops immediately to the bottom. But water splashes around the point of impact. The marble remains intact, while the surface of the water is changed in an instant.

As soon as it hits the water, the marble creates a crater, similar to the one made by a large meteorite striking the surface of the earth. As water is highly malleable, the walls of the crater rise up quickly, becoming thinner and thinner until drops spray out like a rain of precious stones. They drop down and melt into the liquid while the walls of the crater diminish. The bottom of the

Magic from the simplest of events

crater hollows out until, like a volcano, a fluid column grows in the center.

The marble appears at the top of this liquid obelisk, then detaches from it, remaining immobile, lost for 1/1,000th of a second in the immensity of this miniature ocean. It then falls back into the water and drops to the bottom.

The magic is over. The marble dropped at a speed of 15 mph, for a trajectory barely one-half of a second long. If the marble fell at 25 mph, the walls of the crater would have risen higher, and it would have closed in on itself, creating a small air bubble. This often occurs during a rainstorm, when a raindrop falls into a puddle.

This vision of our universe can be provided only by a high-speed photograph, with an exposure time of 20 microseconds. By studying this type of phenomenon, scientists of fluid mechanics research the movement of gases or liquids.

1

3

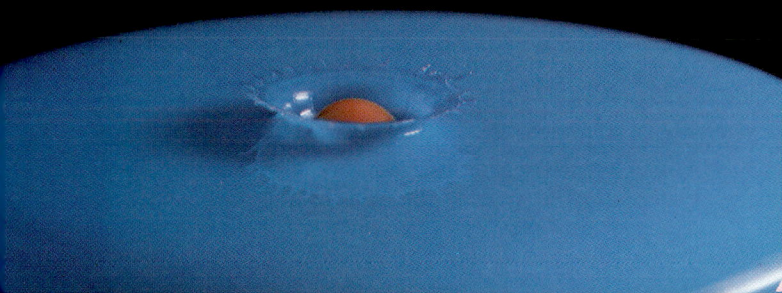

2

4

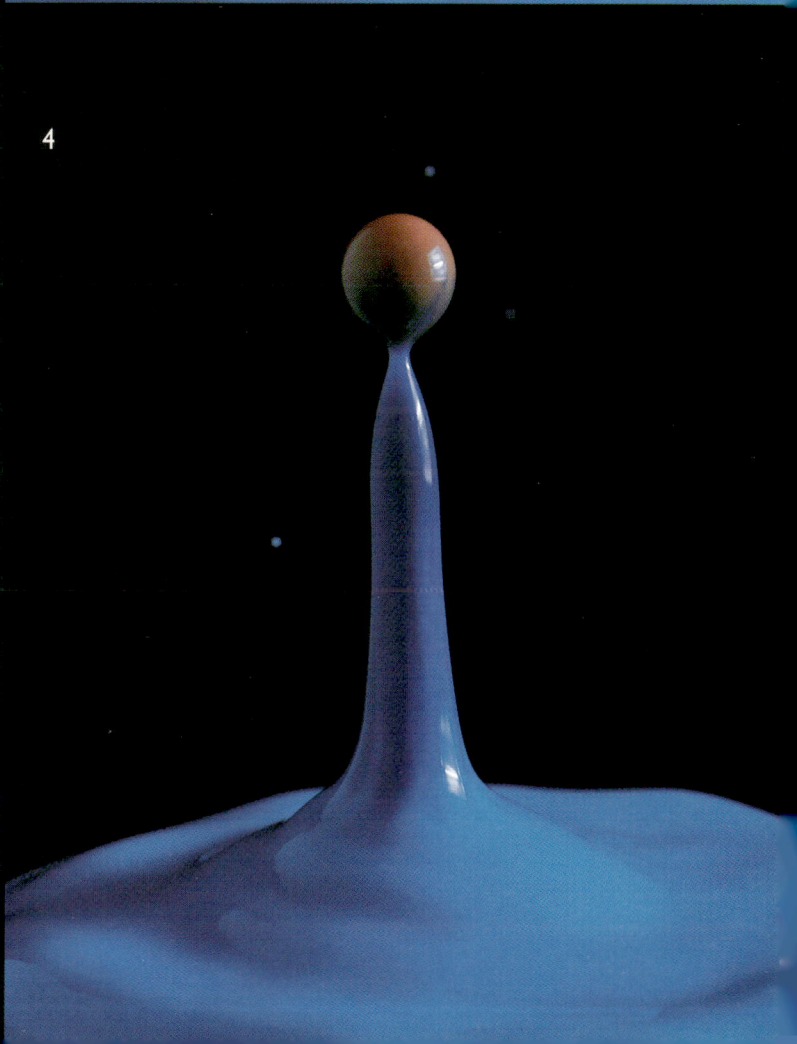

The moment of truth

All the tricks of the trade, all the cameras, and all the techniques work toward a single purpose: to capture the fateful moment, the second the runner's foot leaves the starting block, the instant the swallow drops the worm it carries to its fledglings, or the moment a missile flies in front of the camera, at several hundreds of feet per second. Infrared sensors, photographic cells, and high-speed cameras are the fundamental tools of explorers in the worlds of the incredibly fast.

A moment of inattention and the image is lost! There's nothing to be done; time continues to move in a linear direction. The next photograph will not be exactly alike. Drops of water remain in suspension for a fraction of a second only.

RECORDING DANGER

The world is a dangerous place. When a missile must be fired at speeds of several hundreds of feet per second, it's a good idea to test it before firing. Any small defect could cause a deadly explosion. A misplaced particle at the tip of the firing tube could knock the missile off its course. It would then miss its target, perhaps injuring or killing innocent people in the process. Tests are expensive both in terms of manpower and equipment, and ideal firing conditions are hard to find. Photographs of these events and others, such as stunts, must be obtained on the first shot; there is rarely enough time or money for a second try. Everyone must be ready, most of all the filmmaker or the photographer. If the moment can be programmed, an automatic camera will work much better than a man depending on his reflexes only. Yet this is not always true. Trial runs are often used to prepare a shot.

The countdown for a launch or firing, or the final rehearsal of a stunt scene, provides useful information for the placement of cameras and the timing. Stuntmen like Remy Julienne, who performed the stunts in the most recent James Bond films, never leaves his exploits to chance. Although experience is his most important asset, the precision of the action is such that it requires extraordinary preparation. With his son Dominique, Remy Julienne has developed a software program for stunts. By using the data collected from high-speed films of automobile crashes and wind tunnel tests, he can try out a stunt as if he were actually performing it. Depending on the sequence and its duration, he can therefore determine the speed of the cars and the exact moment of an explosion or fire. He tells the film director at which point the most exciting moments will take place and indicates the best camera angles.

January 28, 1986. Cape Canaveral, Florida. Just 73 seconds after the space shuttle Challenger was launched, it exploded in midair in front of millions of unbelieving viewers. What caused this explosion? Combustion or the booster joints? Without a film of the explosion, the experts would not have been able to determine the cause of this disaster.

One second later and the picture is lost!

ANIMAL FLIGHT

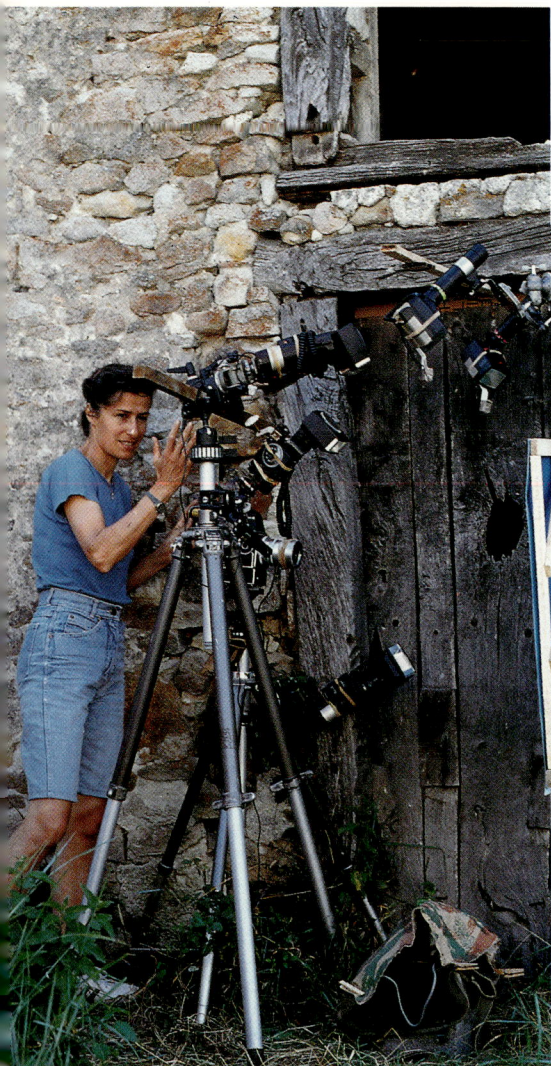

Painstaking preparation and technique are required to capture animals on film. In general, a photographer spends several days observing the animal in its natural habitat. When he can't bring the animal to the studio, he has to set up his equipment in the wild, without raising the suspicions of his subjects.

Birds are best photographed when they are building nests. After setting up the various flash devices along the path the bird follows, the photog-rapher leaves it alone for a few days so that it gets used to the equipment. When the bird's flight is again natural, the photograph can be taken. The photographer, concealed at a distance, triggers his camera with a remote control device; a fully automatic system is even better. In this case, the bird itself triggers the sequence by crossing the light beam of a photoelectric cell. An electronic clock starts operating and controls the flash devices and camera shutter.

Photographing animals in their natural habitats takes careful planning. To capture this swallow in flight, the photographer stretched a thread across the hole in a door. When the bird flew in, the camera was triggered.

The thrill of viewing an invisible event

By using techniques such as electronic traps and by forcing a bird to fly to a preselected place, we can have front-row seats at a fateful moment, watching a kingfisher as it dives and creates effervescence in the water. It is a moment of rare intensity.

Miller Residence

The Miller residence is of considerable architectural interest. The basic structure is a wood frame with clapboard siding. However, the windows and wall edges have been accentuated by further wood relief based on the clapboard geometry. More embellishments are added to the roof eaves. A verandah has unfortunately been removed from the front elevation; however the building is witness to the high quality of wood craftsmanship prevalent in the late nineteenth century of the County.
Location: Part of Lot 30, Con. 10

The best photographic conditions are those created by the photographer himself. When possible, he constructs a small studio outside to capture the lightning-fast dive of a kingfisher.

THE PREY AND THE PREDATOR

The movements of animals are often determined by their instinct for survival. A potential prey is constantly on the lookout for danger, and its reaction time must be faster than that of its predator. The predator knows this and may pretend to be interested in something else before it leaps on its prey. Some animals, such as birds of prey, use speed as their primary weapon. The chameleon, however, waits for its prey to come within striking distance. As soon as it is in sight, the chameleon's colors intensify. It freezes, with all senses alert, contracting its sticky tongue. It then starts to push it out slightly, keeping the insect in view. A dual movement involving the bones and muscles of the tongue push this formidable weapon 8 inches forward in just 1/20th of a second, capturing the insect, which sticks to the chameleon's tongue. Less than a quarter of a second later, it has retracted its tongue, and the insect has been swallowed!

This technique is not foolproof. Insects have their own resources. They generally fly at speeds of 7 to 30 feet per second; the dragonfly can even reach a speed of 58 feet per second. Others, such as locusts, can fly or jump. These insects do not usually fly, but their strong legs can propel them to great heights. They can jump up to 35 times their own height (for a person 5'6" tall, this is the equivalent of jumping as high as a 15-story building). When they can no longer find anything to eat, they move to another area.

Locusts live in groups and travel in enormous flying clouds ready to land and devastate the land lying below. Their wings, which are usually not very strong and not able to carry them very far, grow longer, and they can fly over entire continents. They save their energy by flying in close formation, reducing the air resistance, landing to ravage entire crops along their path.

The English photographer Stephen Dalton specialized in shots of small animals. He constructed a complete device with flash equipment, photoelectric cell, camera, and electronic clock. Even the path of the insects was planned. By controlling all the technical variables of the photograph, he captured the elusive image in his ministudio.

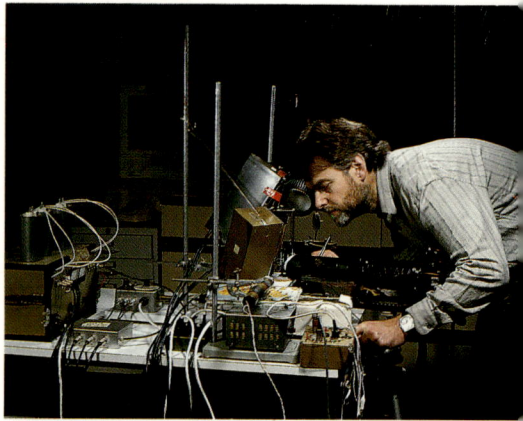

The coup de grace is over in a second.

Locusts move at incredibly fast speeds. Photographed in the tunnel created by Stephen Dalton, in which a natural environment is re-created, this image represents 1/25,000th of a second in the life of a migratory locust.

SWANS AND HUMMINGBIRDS

The hummingbird, on the other hand, is a marvel of strength and flexibility in flight. Its wings are particularly well balanced, and its strong frame is perfect for its weight. The ball-and-socket shoulder joint allows the bird to flap its wings up to 80 times per second, making it the swiftest bird in the world.

This agility also means that it is a solitary breed. As opposed to the swan, which only flies in formation, the hummingbird is not concerned with air resistance. The weight of the swan is close to the upper limit to allow flight; the hummingbird's is so low, however, that its wingspan and muscular structure are more than sufficient for its movements.

There are thousands of different species of birds, and each one has its own unique style and speed of flight. Some prefer to glide in the prevailing winds; others, the majority, flap their wings to move forward and cause a difference in pressure above and below the wings, creating enough uplift to keep them in the air. The weight, the wing surface, and the muscular structure are the determining factors in a bird's flight and speed.

The swan and the hummingbird represent the two extremes. One is extraordinarily graceful and the other extremely dexterous. The swan has large, powerful wings but encounters difficulty in taking off. Ideally, it should weigh less, because the wing surface is proportional to the weight of the bird, a fact that aircraft designers learned early on. This is the heart of the swan's problem. It has a wingspan of over 8 feet, and its strong frame has to work hard to lift its 26 pounds. It almost walks across the water in an effort to gain speed, and it takes a fairly long time before it lifts off. It flaps its wings frantically. Swans are beautiful in flight, graceful and elongated. They fly in formation to reduce air resistance.

High-speed recording serves two purposes. First, it can capture movements such as the rapid wing movements of the hummingbird. It can also break down slow movements, such as those of the swan.

When a swan wants to land, it contracts its body. The long tail feathers form an air brake. Its alula, the short feathers on the leading edge of the wings, are raised and help to stabilize the bird. After a series of splashes, frantic wing flapping, and rebounds, the bird finally lands.

Iridescent colors for an energetic bird

It has been called an insect-bird because its wings flap so quickly: up to 80 beats per second. The hummingbird's amazing virtuosity in flight is almost acrobatic. It can fly forward, of course, but also backward, the only bird able to do so. It can also hover in a stationary position as it feeds on flower nectar.

ATHLETES REVEAL THEIR SECRETS

Intensive training, assessment of an athlete's physiology, and meticulous analyses of performance and physical conditions: Trainers and equipment manufacturers depend on visual images of specific movements in their persistent efforts to improve athletic results. Every high-level athlete and every sporting goods manufacturer depends on the information provided by high-speed photography.

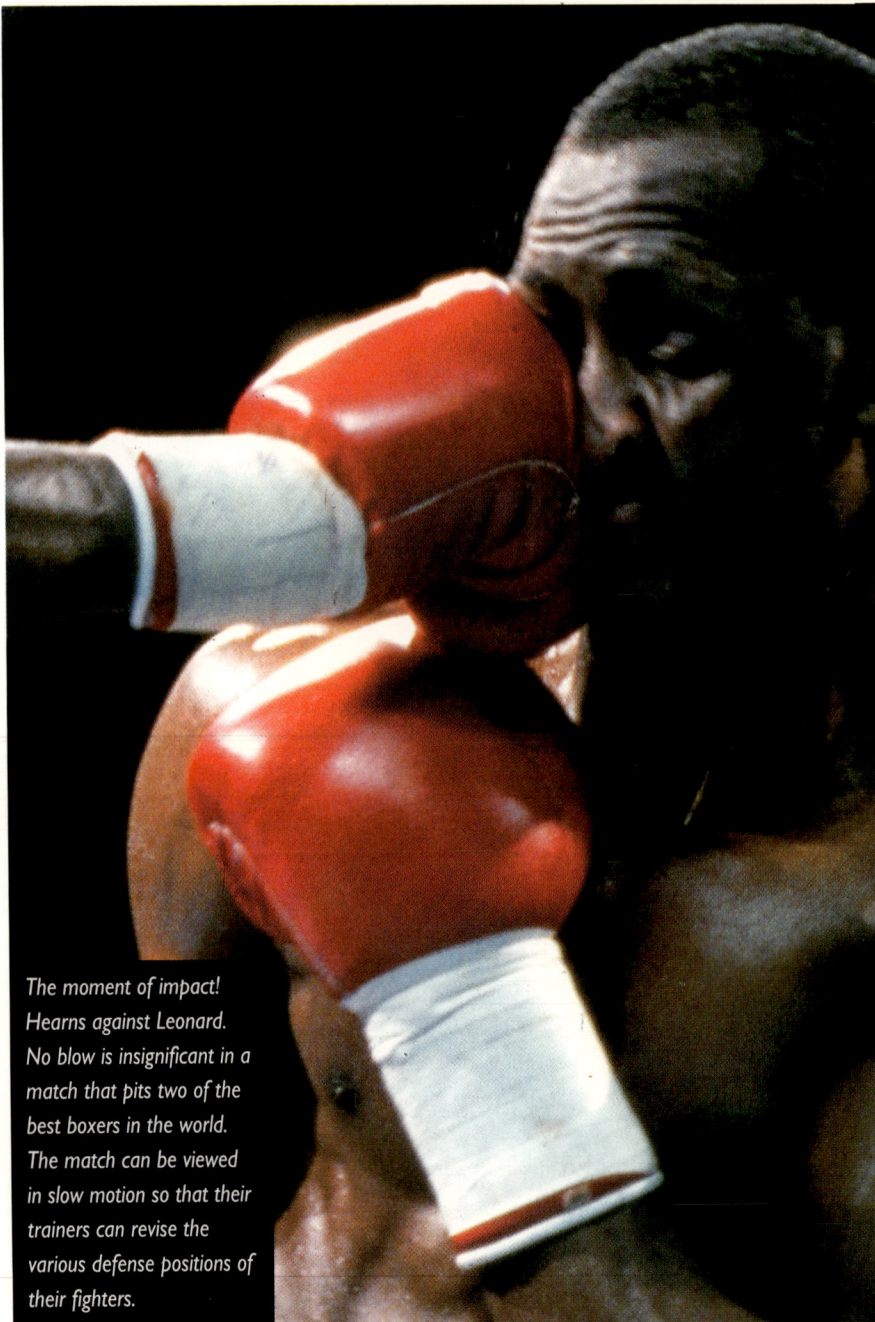

The moment of impact! Hearns against Leonard. No blow is insignificant in a match that pits two of the best boxers in the world. The match can be viewed in slow motion so that their trainers can revise the various defense positions of their fighters.

At the end of the game the athletes review their performance in slow motion. This cinematographic technique, invented by Lucien Bull and Henri Nogues in 1904, reveals every movement of an athlete. Edwin Moses, the world record-holder in the 400-meter hurdles, uses film as an important tool in his training. As do most of his adversaries! By studying his stride, he can determine the best way to reduce the number of steps taken and to run faster.

At the French National Institute for Physical Education and Sports, the trainers film their athletes at a speed of 4,000 frames per second. In research laboratories, the gait of a person walking and the body movements are studied. A platform is connected to a high-speed video, which can measure the different pressures exerted by the muscles. In turn, this data provides information concerning the correct conditions for walking, in which the optimum energy expenditure is attained.

Sporting goods manufacturers have followed this trend closely. To improve performance, they have learned how to create equipment that is best suited to the athlete's body: clothing (especially shoes), poles, tennis rackets, and golf clubs. A difference in the position of the center of gravity in a golf club, its shape, or the shape of the ball will result in a different shot for the same player. With a flash timed to 1/100,000th of a second, we can see the extraordinary impact of a racket as it smashes into a ball, transmitting to it enough energy to propel it across the court.

A tennis ball, struck with enough force to send it across the court at 124 mph, nears the racket at a speed of 74.5 mph. At the moment of impact, it compresses and flattens out in an effort to pass through the holes of the racket. The strings stretch, bending the racket frame, which resists and absorbs the stress. The strings cushion the energy of the shot, slowing down the ball and stopping it in the space of a thousandth of a second. It then retightens and pushes the ball back in the opposite direction. The energy transmitted to the ball deforms it again. It looks like an egg with the point toward the front. The rear edge catches up to it, and it returns to its spherical shape.

Photographic impact

Understanding comes through observation. Explosions, detonations, high-speed impacts, and shattering are physical processes so rapid that the only way to understand them is to break down the event into slower and shorter fragments. Filming the Ariane missile, which opens its cap at a speed of several miles per second, or collision tests requested by automobile companies to improve safety conditions requires special high-speed film and photographic equipment.

During a stunt, in which the slow motion is only two to five times less than the actual time of the stunt, it is a good idea to understand the properties of a material before attempting the exploit. This motorcycle breaks through a brick wall and shatters it; bricks fly off as if caught in a ferocious cyclone.

FASTER THAN AIR TURBULENCE

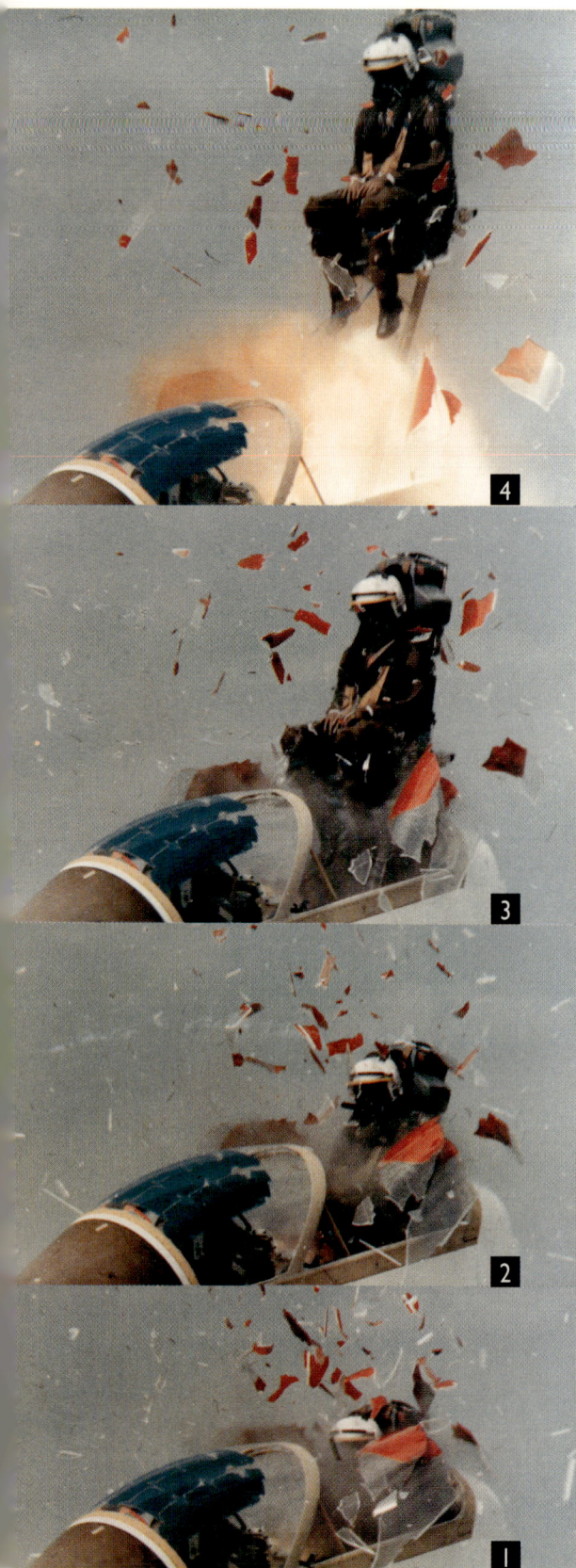

An airplane is about to crash to the ground. The pilot triggers his ejection seat. The glass of his cockpit explodes, and he is projected up and out. When his head leaves the cockpit, he is in the full force of the wind because he is still moving at the speed of the airplane. Due to the correct design and positioning of the seat and pilot, the wind does not propel him backward. Tests of this equipment are not conducted in flight as they would be too costly. Instead, a moving model traveling at Mach 1.5 (1,118 mph) is used. High-speed cameras film the programmed scene. When this pilot of a MIG-29 (below) was ejected at a French airport on June 8, 1989, he had to be sure to trigger his release at the right moment.

We have come a long way from the early days of the airplane and the automobile. Accidents still exist, however. In France alone there are more than 200,000 people injured and 10,000 killed per year on the roads. Airplane crashes, although seldom, also occur. Nevertheless, the number would be much higher without "scratch tests," during which manufacturers observe the behavior of every part of an automobile. They can then add safety measures or reinforce sections. Approximately 400 of these tests are conducted every year, 200 of which involve the entire car.

Current safety measures favor the use of the air bag, which is installed in the steering wheel and inflates on impact. A "pretightener" is also undergoing tests. This is a system in which the seat belt is blocked faster and restrains the passenger more quickly.

When a car moving at 62 mph hits a stationary car, the following sequence takes place: At the point of impact, the fenders touch and crash together at the same instant as the front body and the headlights, which explode in a shower of glass. Just 0.02 seconds later, the motors, made of much harder material, meet head on. At 0.025 seconds after the crash, the driver is projected toward the windshield. At 0.03 seconds, the seat belt tightens on its pulley, and the belt pulls out. The man is still moving forward. The motors are still crashing together. At 0.05 seconds the belt has reached its limit. The man bounces backward, while the car still moves forward. At 0.08 seconds, the two motors have absorbed all the energy of the impact. The car has stopped. At 0.1 seconds, the man moves forward slightly. At 0.12 seconds, he again moves backward and is stabilized. At 0.13 seconds, the crash is over. The passenger area is intact.

Working to make machines safe

FASTER THAN HIS SHADOW

Only Lucky Luke can fire faster than his own shadow. The dream of exceeding the speed of light has not yet been reached, but high-speed imaging is close: It can actually freeze a bullet in midair. Some "fly" at more than 2,700 feet per second (1,860 mph). In slow motion, we can begin to understand this world of speed. In 1919, Lucien Bull succeeded in filming a bullet going through a wood plank at 13,000 frames per second.

Harold Edgerton, who invented the strobe light, was the first to record the surprising image of a bullet smashing as it hits a steel plate. The bullet heats up very quickly when it reaches the target. It deforms at the same time as the metal, liquefies, and seems to be welded to the plate. It digs an impact crater, perforates the plate, then gradually returns to its initial form. It continues along its path, although it has lost a great deal of energy in the form of heat.

To film these events and others, such as high-speed ballistics tests, the military has developed special cameras. They have mirrors on three sides, which turn at more than 4,000 revolutions per second. The reflections of the event successively sweep across a hundred lenses, which capture the images. These cameras can therefore record a record-breaking several million frames per second.

The prototype of high-speed imaging: A bullet from a .22 caliber gun, traveling at more than 992 mph, cuts lengthwise through a playing card. The bullet has cut the card, but the bottom part has not yet fallen. High-speed imaging has created even more astonishing images. It is often used to analyze missiles as they leave launch tubes. The Hot 2, for example, leaves the tube at 230 feet per second and accelerates at an astonishing speed, reaching 820 feet per second in only 12 yards.

At the far right side of the image, a rifle bullet is frozen at a speed of more than 800 mph. Three balloons lie in its path. By exposing the film for 1/2,000,000th of a second, the various stages of their bursting can be observed. Another balloon explodes, and the talcum powder with which it was filled retains its shape for a brief instant.

Missiles and bullets, propelled by an explosive chemical reaction and faster than an animal in flight, are usually visible only when they reach their targets. A film of their trajectories, however, provides a record of their brief, destructive lives and an image of their impact.

AN EXPLOSIVE MOMENT

I f we could observe the world at a speed of one-millionth of a second, we would be astonished by the beauty of the physical processes that take place in the heart of matter. When a laser excites atoms or when a projectile strikes its target, the effect is not instantaneous. In Japan X-ray cameras are being developed; these have exposure times of approximately 0.5 nanoseconds. There is one problem, however; the exposure time is so short that photographers have to use incredibly powerful flash devices.

At the Saint-Gobain plant, glass is formed and stress tests are conducted on the finished items, which include bottles, windows, windshields, light bulbs, and other products. Before safety standards were changed, car windshields were made of .2-inch-thick tempered glass; when they broke, they shattered into small, .08-inch-long pieces. Now, however, safety standards require that all manufacturers equip cars with windshields made of laminated glass. Tests have demonstrated the effects of impact as, for example, when a 1.28-inch ball is dropped from a height of 11.5 feet onto a windshield.

The glass breaks at the first contact. The pieces hit by the ball push the others to the side, and a small, .08-inch crater is formed in the middle. This resembles the crater caused by a marble dropped into water (see page 18). The inner part has been turned to dust and looks like sugar crystals. Cracks appear from these edges, which follow the curve of the glass and extend to the areas of least resistance.

An explosion is a sudden liberation of gas and energy. But the gas is not always present. Explosions may also be caused by an impact between materials, when one of the materials cannot withstand the force of the other. This occurs with glass, which breaks into a thousand pieces under the impact of a projectile or as a result of high heat.

Windshields, which consist of two sheets of glass of different thicknesses laminated together with plastic resin, splinter into shards measuring 2.7 to 3.12 inches long by .2 inch wide.

For an instant

projectile and target seem to be bonded.

The impact lasts one-millionth of a second. The projectile pushes the glass barrier; the light bulb cannot contain the tension created. At the moment the bulb bursts, the vacuum and gas inside create a high pressure, increasing the effect of the explosion.

NATURE MOVES FASTER THAN WE THINK

During chemical, nuclear, or physical reactions, nature possesses unsuspected resources to produce or liberate energy and this often results in tremendous explosions. The effects are fast and violent, as with the energy of a volcano, a meteorological phenomenon such as a cyclone, or the even more powerful release that occurs in the core of a star. Man has tried to tame and re-create these voraciously destructive energies.

In England, scientists started copying the strongest and most secret energy of the sun: thermonuclear fusion. Certain hydrogen atoms are compressed by a magnetic field. In so doing, they bond for several thousandths of a second, forming heavier atoms. Part of their mass is transformed into energy, the same energy that is produced by the sun and that lights our days, provides heat, and allows the existence of life.

Man is only in the early stages of his experiments. Nonetheless, mechanical, chemical, and more recently nuclear energies have been more or less tamed by mankind. New techniques are most often developed by the military, which has extremely sophisticated high-speed observation methods. At the Saint-Louis Franco-German Institute in the Haut-Rhin region, scientists conduct research and development analyses on weapons. Explosions are an everyday occurrence, including liquids or metal walls that explode under the impact of powerful projectiles or lasers. Nuclear bombs are also meticulously analyzed to break down the various steps of the explosion.

The detonation of a nuclear bomb, which occurs faster than the speed of sound, creates a shock wave that compresses and propels the ambient air. A standard camera capable of 25 frames per second is sufficient to capture the image of the rising mushroom cloud. The explosion and the blast, however, require 500 frames per second. The physical reactions in the explosion require equipment capable of capturing 10,000 frames per second.

Physical-chemical reactions

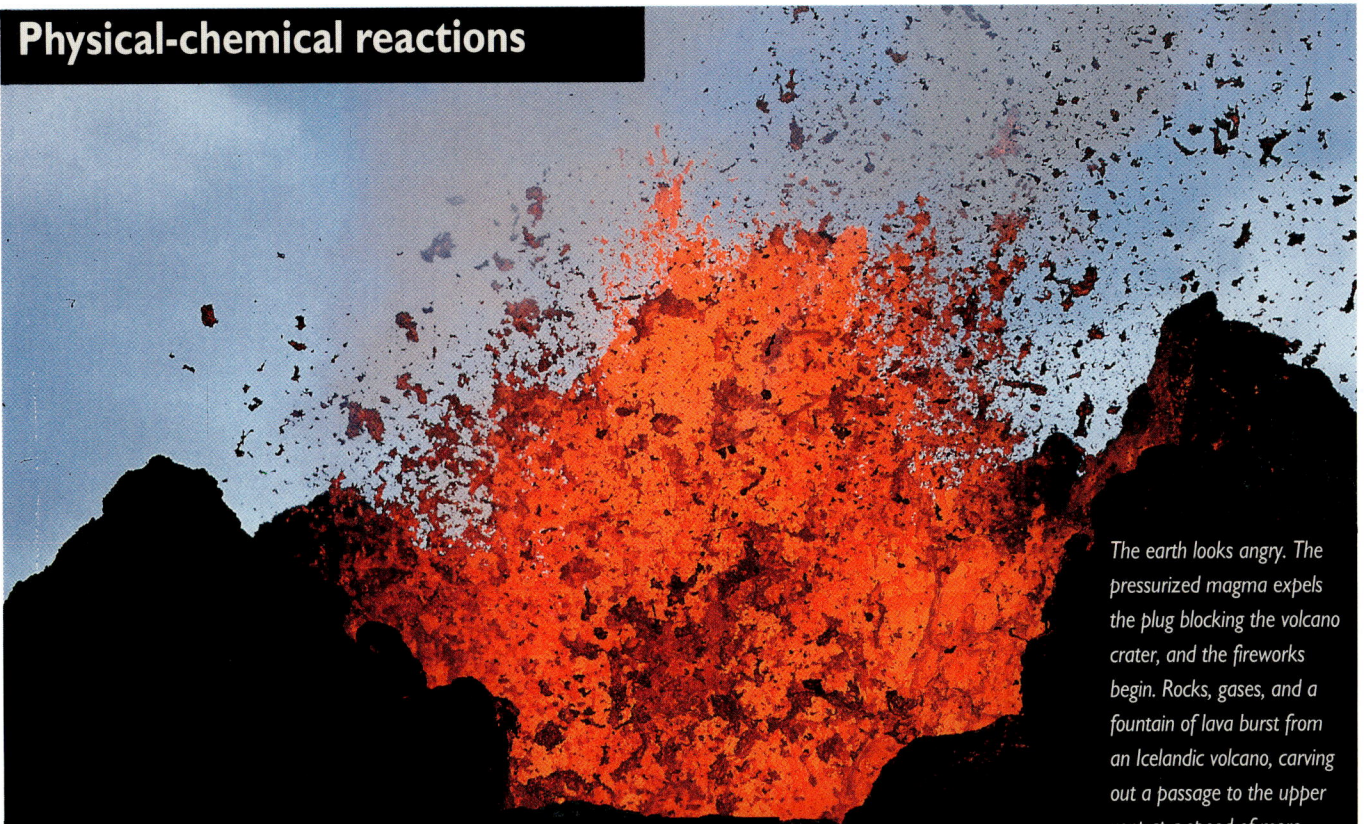

are devastating and fast

The earth looks angry. The pressurized magma expels the plug blocking the volcano crater, and the fireworks begin. Rocks, gases, and a fountain of lava burst from an Icelandic volcano, carving out a passage to the upper vent at a speed of more than 62 mph.

and release enormous energy.

The pressurized gas in a champagne bottle pushes the cork out at 16 feet per second. A stream of bubbles follow, overtaking and accompanying the cork.

Traces of passage are left behind

It is not always possible to observe objects in motion. Sometimes they are too far away or too small or imperceptible, and sometimes they are nothing more than luminous phenomena. Researchers require special equipment to capture the elusive trace of elementary particles in an accelerator, the magic of a fireworks display, or the rush of air alongside a missile.

A PARADE OF PARTICLES

Pushed to the extreme, the movements of objects are no longer recorded; it is the trace they leave behind that is registered. The light emitted during chemical or nuclear reactions provide physicists with enough information to reconstruct the movements of particles of matter and to reveal the secrets of this miniature fireworks display.

A photon, or particle of light, travels 600 million miles an hour. A particle of matter accelerated by an intense magnetic field strikes a target at several hundreds of thousands of miles per hour. These are too fleeting and too small to be observed directly. In the large particle accelerators, such as those of the CERN (European Center of Nuclear Research) near Geneva, high-speed film techniques are used, not to detect the passage of these phantom bits of matter, but to observe the traces they leave behind.

Most of the experiments are designed to add to our understanding of the nature and quantity of particles. When matter and antimatter (an electron and a positron) are brought together, when an "event" takes place, as it is known by the physicists, a colossal amount of energy is released in the form of a particle with an infinitesimally short life. This then disintegrates into a rain of numerous lighter particles. Before 1980 the particle detectors used were called bubble chambers, cloud chambers, and spark chambers. The electrically charged particles struck atoms that ionized; in other words, they also became charged. The entire event was recorded on photographic film. The only problem was that detectors process up to 50,000 collisions per second. These methods were not suitable for rapid computer analysis, which can reconstruct the trajectory of particles and their positrons to within 1/270,000th of an inch.

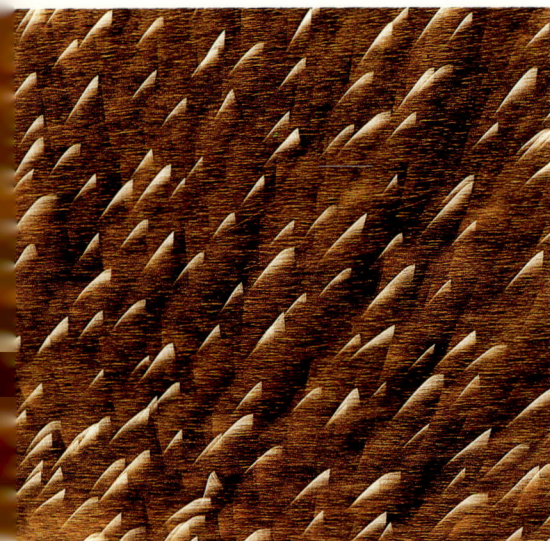

Explosive chemical reactions produce an enormous quantity of light. This one, because of its color, indicates the density of the energy emitted and the type of atoms that participated in the event. Fireworks designers control this phenomenon to create a series of reactions that explode over the heads of delighted spectators.

In the chemical reactions that occur with fireworks, excited atoms emit light. In physics, certain particles, such as neutrinos, do not interact with matter. Scientists can determine their energetic properties only by studying the trajectory and the nature of other particles created.

When an electrified sulfur
atom strikes a target of
gold at several thousands of
miles per second, a shower
of particles bursts forth.
They cannot be seen with
the naked eye, but in
reaction with the gas in a
streamer chamber, they
emit electrons whose trails
can be recorded.

PHOTOGRAPHING THE INVISIBLE

Marey faced the question years ago: How can photographers capture the image of airflows when they are transparent? How to correct motor or aircraft wing vibrations, detectable by the ear but imperceptible to the eye? In 1900 Marey had the idea of using small blasts of white smoke, which deviated when they came in contact with an object.

This was the prototype for modern wind tunnels. Smoke has been replaced by small particles, and technology and optic theory have provided different methods.

These techniques—ombroscopy, strioscopy, holography, or interferometry—are all based on the optical deviations of fluids and gases. Depending on its density, air acts as a lens, a prism, or a telescope. By observing the areas of shadow and light, the movement of air around missiles and the path of combustion gases can be reconstructed. The display of turbulence, shock, compression, or expansion waves, as well as the airstream behind the projectile, is obtained in the same way.

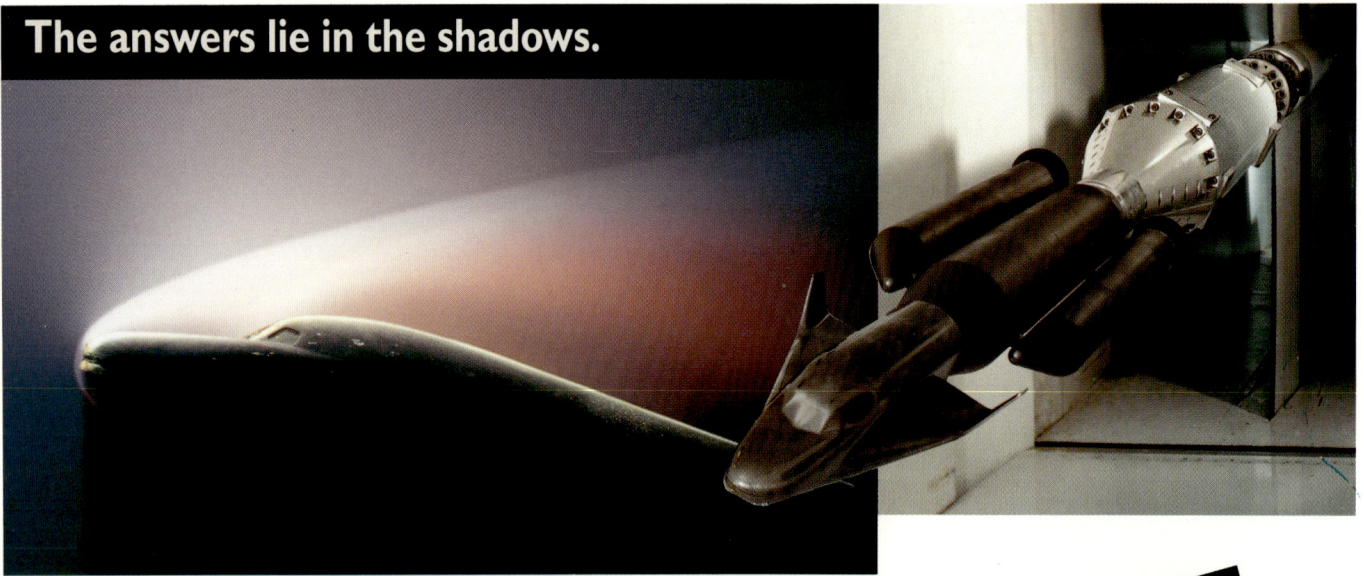

The answers lie in the shadows.

This European spacecraft may never be constructed, but its model has withstood blasts of air at speeds of 7,440 mph in wind tunnels. The airflow is displayed by a beam of electrons that hits molecules of air, making them fluorescent and therefore luminous. Vibrations of the Ariane 5 launcher are also tested.

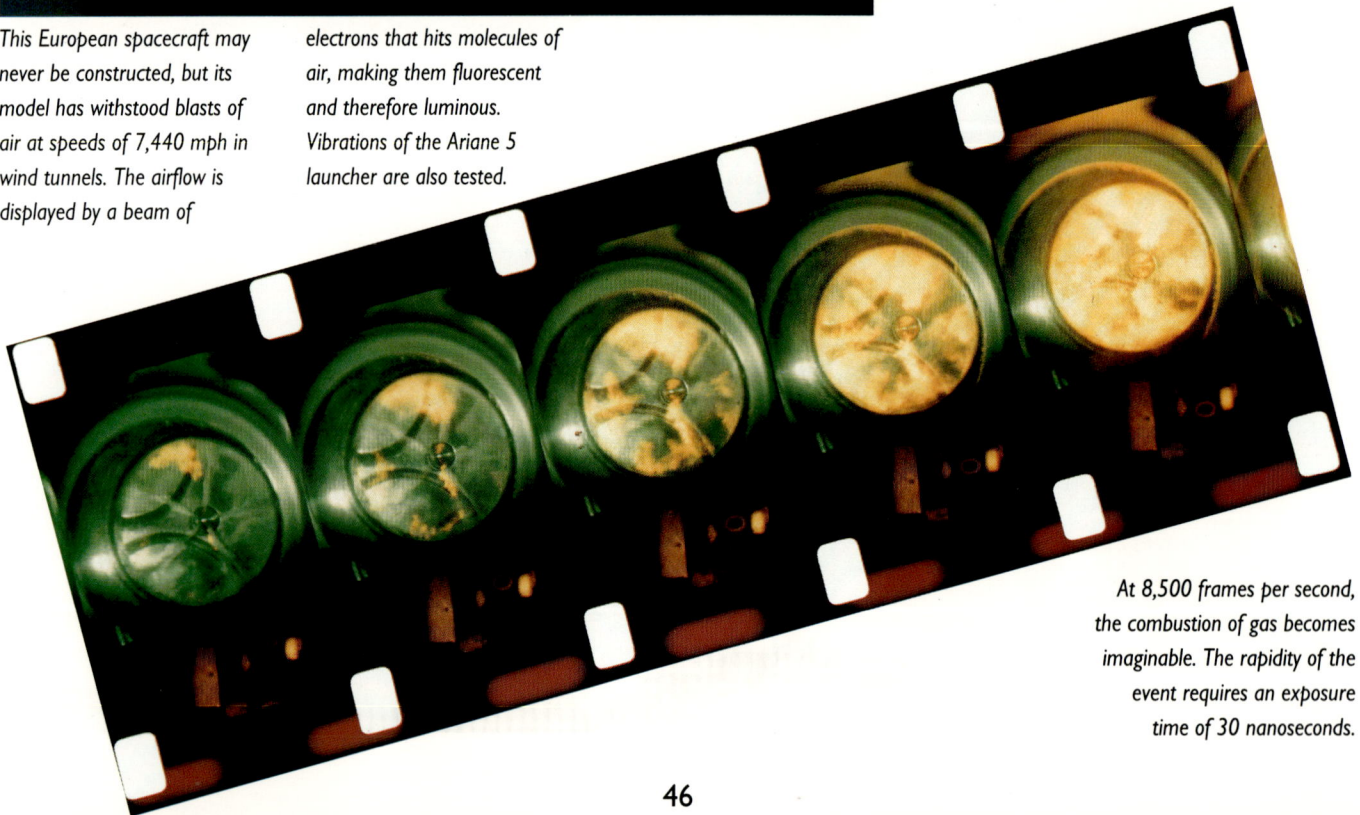

At 8,500 frames per second, the combustion of gas becomes imaginable. The rapidity of the event requires an exposure time of 30 nanoseconds.

Ombroscopy is the technique most commonly used to visualize the movement of air because it is one of the easiest to use. When an iron arrow hits at 5,900 feet per second, its form creates turbulence that modifies the air density. The flash lasts less than a microsecond. The light, coming from behind, travels more slowly through the denser layer, which then appears darker in the image. This method is often used in ballistics.

Photo Credits

P. 2: © Musée Marey, Beaune. P. 2–3: © CNRS de Poitiers, laboratoire de métallurgie physique. P. 4: © Collège de France. P. 5: © Jean-Loup Charmet. P. 6–7: © A. Visage/ Bios. P. 7: © Nature. P. 8: © François Cherrier (top left), © A. Visage/ Bios (bottom left), © François Cherrier (right). P. 9: © Harold Edgerton/ Science photo library, Bios. P.10–11: © Marie-Claude et Jean-Gilles Baillet (top), © Dalton/ NHPA, Nature (bottom). P.12–13: © A. Visage/ Bios P. 14–15: © Hervé Chaumeton/ Nature. P. 16: © Hadland Photonics (top left), © Hadland Photonics (top center and right). P. 16–17: © Alain Ernoult P. 17: © IPI (top center). P. 18–19: © Hervé Chaumeton/ Nature. P. 20–21: © Tom Sanders/ Adventures Photo. P. 21: © Alain Ernoult. P. 22: © David Welcher/ Sygma (center), © Guichard/ Gamma (left), © Jones/ Gamma (right). P. 23: © Alain Ernoult. P. 24: © Marie-Claude et Jean-Gilles Baillet. P. 25: © Marie-Claude et Jean-Gilles Baillet. P. 26: © Stephen Dalton/ NHPA. P. 27: © Stephen Dalton/ NHPA. P. 28: © M. Danegger/ Jacana. P. 29: © R. Seitre/ Bios. P. 30: L'Equipe/ Sport. P. 31: © DR. P.32–33: © Alain Ernoult. P. 33: © Alain Ernoult. P. 34: © Crown A & AEE Boscombe Down (left), © Eddy Guilloux/ ADIP (right). P. 35: © Eddy Guilloux. P. 36: © G. Settles & S. Mcintyre/ Science photo library, Cosmos. P. 37: © Science photo library/ Cosmos (top), © J. Watts/ Science photo library/ Cosmos. P. 38: © Philip K. Sharpe/ Oxford scientific films. P. 39: © Zefa. P. 40: © Gamma (left), © C. Vioujard/ Gamma (right). P. 41: © Explorer (top), Jonathan Watts & Peter Parks/ Oxford scientific library, Fovéa. P. 42–43: © Keith Kent. P. 44: © Dirk Reinartz/ Cosmos (left), © DR (right). P. 45: © CERN Genève. P. 46: © ONERA (top left), © ONERA (top right), © Eric Laugh/ UMSIT Manchester (bottom). P. 47: © ISL.

Front Cover: © Arold Edgerton / Camera Press; © Imapress. Back Cover: © CNRS de Poitiers, laboratoire de métallurgie physique.

Design and layout: Etienne Hénocq - François Huertas.

New Discovery Books
Macmillan Publishing Company
866 Third Avenue
New York, NY 10022

Maxwell Macmillan Canada, Inc.
1200 Eglinton Avenue East
Suite 200
Don Mills, Ontario M3C 3N1

Macmillan Publishing Company is part of the Maxwell Communication Group of Companies.

First Edition
Printed in the United States of America
10 9 8 7 6 5 4 3 2 1

ISBN 0-02-708435-3
Library of Congress Catalog Card Number 93-462